Contents

My name is Lily. I am eight years old.
I live in New York City.
New York City is a very big city with lots of
yellow taxis and very tall skyscrapers.

a city

a taxi

a skyscraper

5

In New York City, there are many things to see. Some of the most famous places are the Empire State Building, the Statue of Liberty and Central Park.

the Empire
State Building

the Statue
of Liberty

Central Park

My favorite place is Central Park. I go roller skating there with my mom. I love the beautiful trees and lakes in the park. Many New Yorkers go to the park for picnics.

a park

roller skating

my mom

a tree

a lake

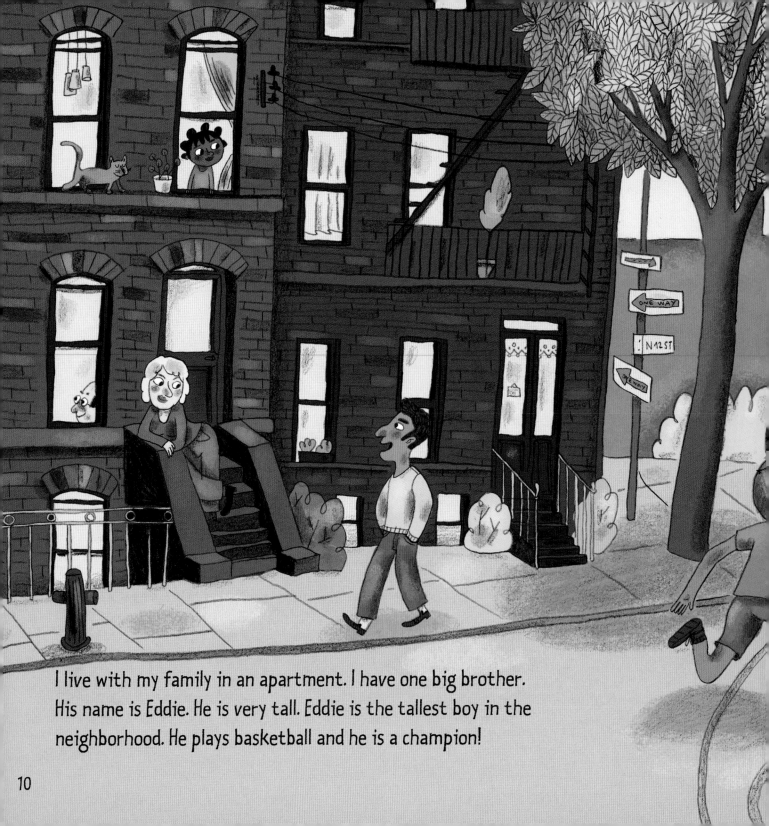

I live with my family in an apartment. I have one big brother.
His name is Eddie. He is very tall. Eddie is the tallest boy in the
neighborhood. He plays basketball and he is a champion!

my family

an apartment

my brother

tall/short

basketball

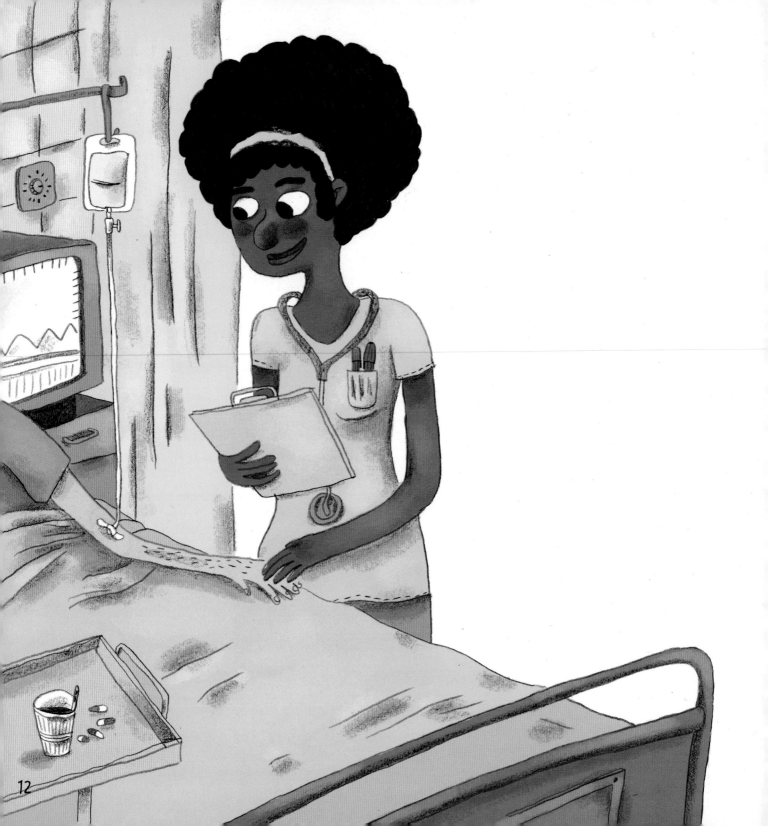

My mom is a nurse. She helps people who are sick.
My dad is a captain on a ferryboat. He takes people
around the harbor of New York City.
I love my parents!

a nurse

sick

my dad

a ferryboat

a harbor

We have a dog. His name is Foxy.
Foxy loves to eat cookies and milk. Do you like cookies?

a dog

cookies

milk

15

I walk to school every day. My teacher is Mrs. Robinson.
She teaches math, writing, reading and spelling.
Spelling is my favorite subject and I love spelling bees!

FANTASTI...

my school

my teacher

math

writing

reading

H.O.M._

spelling bees

My best friend is Madison. She loves to read books.
She wants to be an astronaut.
At recess we play hopscotch and double dutch.
It's fun!

my friends

a book

an astronaut

hopscotch

double dutch

On Saturdays, I take painting lessons at the
Museum of Modern Art.
I love looking at the beautiful paintings.

to paint

the Museum of Modern Art

a painting

to look at

I have a musical family.
I play the violin. My brother plays the banjo.
My dad plays the harmonica. My mom plays the piano.
And the neighbors dance!

a violin

a banjo

a harmonica

a piano

the neighbors

My mom is a great cook. My favorite meal is Sunday brunch.
We eat pancakes with maple syrup, fruit, jelly, bacon and eggs.
It is yummy!

a cook

pancakes

jelly

bacon

an egg

25

In October, we celebrate Halloween.
Everyone wears a costume and there are jack-o-lanterns everywhere.
We go trick-or-treating to all the houses in the neighborhood.
The neighbors put lots of candy in our baskets.
How many jack-o-lanterns do you see?

a costume

a house

a candy

trick-or-treat

a jack-o-lantern

At Thanksgiving, we drive to Washington, D. C. to see my grandma and grandpa. We visit the White House where the President of the United States of America lives with his family. One day, I would like to meet the President.

my grandma

my grandpa

the United States
of America

the White House

That's it! The visit is over!
I hope to see you soon in New York City. Bye bye!

Bye bye!